Contents

The Fall and the Rise of a Merchant

There once lived a very successful merchant in a prosperous kingdom. He was famous for his generosity and fairness. The king was impressed with him and made him the kingdom's administrator.

The merchant organised a grand wedding for his daughter. He invited the king and the queen, and other prominent people of the royal court.

While the merchant was busy attending to the royal guests, a servant of the royal household came and sat on a seat that was meant only for nobles. When the merchant saw him, he became furious. He scolded the servant and asked him to leave. The servant felt offended. He didn't sleep all night and planned his revenge.

The next morning, the servant was sweeping the courtyard when he saw the king taking a morning stroll.

He acted as if he was half asleep and mumbled, "Look at the audacity of the merchant! He embraced the queen. Lord, save him!"

The king heard him and asked him sternly, "You! Come here! Did you see the merchant embrace the queen?"

The servant pleaded, "My Lord, I got no sleep last night. Forgive me. I must be talking in my sleep."

The king didn't answer, but the servant knew that the seed of distrust had been sown.

The king became suspicious. He decided to bar the merchant from the royal household. Thus, when the merchant came to visit the king, he was not allowed to enter. The servant saw him arguing with the palace guards and teased him, "Guards! This merchant is a mighty person. He could get you arrested for your rude behaviour."

The merchant understood that it had been the servant's trick. He acted maturely and decided to resolve things with the servant. He did not want to fall out of the king's grace permanently.

The same day, he invited the servant to his house for lunch, gave him several presents, and apologized for his behaviour. The servant was delighted and accepted the apology. He said, "Don't worry. I will ensure that the king starts trusting you again."

The next day, while sweeping the king's room, the servant saw the king half-awake.

He again mumbled, "Our king has a secret! He eats cucumber in the bathroom!"

The king became furious and asked, "Are you out of your mind? When did you see me doing that?"

The servant apologised immediately and said, "Forgive me, Lord, I don't know what I have been mumbling in my sleep. I surely need some sleep!"

The king understood that the servant mumbled nonsense, which made him realise that he had been wrong about the merchant too. He invited the merchant to his palace and showered gifts on him.

Moral

We should treat everyone with respect.

The Mice that Ate Iron

Once, a trader wanted to travel to a distant kingdom and needed some funds. So, he went to a merchant he knew. He borrowed some money from the merchant, leaving his iron scales behind as security.

When the trader came back from his trip, he went to the merchant's house. He returned the money he had borrowed and said, "Now you must return the iron scales I had given as security."

The greedy merchant refused and said, "There are so many rats in my shop. They must have eaten your iron scales."

The trader knew that the merchant was lying but didn't argue. He shrugged and said, "Never mind. I brought several bags of silk cloth from my trip. Will you ask your son to come with me so that he can fetch a few bags for you?"

The greedy merchant agreed and asked his son to accompany the trader.

The trader took the boy to a cave and said, "I have stored my goods inside the cave. Could you go inside and bring two bags?"

When the boy went inside the cave, the trader quickly blocked its entrance. He went back to the merchant alone. The worried merchant asked the trader, "Where is my son?"

"I'm sorry, a flamingo took your boy in its claws and flew away," said the trader.

The merchant became furious and said, "I will complain to the elders of the village."

When the village elders asked the trader to tell the truth, the trader replied, "If rats can eat iron, why can't a flamingo carry a boy?"

Confused, the elders asked him to explain the matter. After hearing his story, the elders scolded the merchant and asked him to return the scales.

The trader set the boy free after getting his scales back.

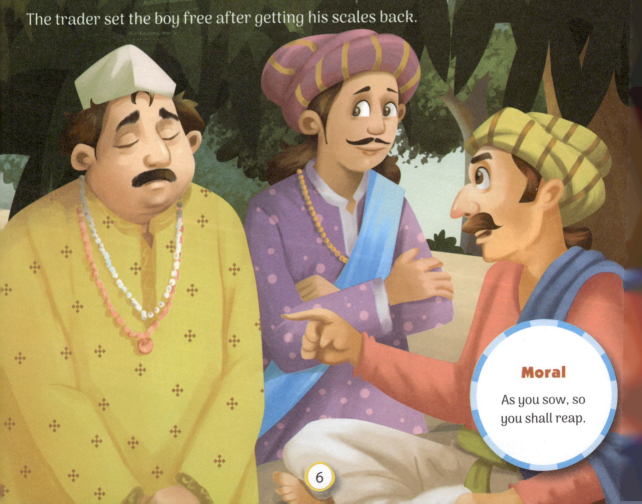

Moral

As you sow, so you shall reap.

The Wolf and the Crane

A wolf was enjoying a nice meal when a bone got stuck in his throat. He was in terrible pain. He tried to take it out several times but failed. He asked his friends for help, but no one could get the bone out. Finally, he went to the crane for help.

"I will give you anything if you take this bone out of my throat," said the wolf.

The crane agreed to help. She asked the wolf to keep his mouth wide open. She put her beak inside the wolf's mouth and pulled out the bone.

When she asked for a reward, the wolf grinned and said, "You placed your head inside a wolf's mouth, and yet you are alive. Isn't that a reward?"

Moral

Don't expect gratitude from wicked people.

The Fox and the Stork

One day, a fox invited his friend, the stork, to dinner. To poke fun at his friend, the fox served soup in a shallow dish. The stork tried to drink the soup but could merely wet the tip of his beak. Meanwhile, the fox grinned and asked, "Didn't you like the soup?"

"I guess I am not hungry," said the stork and left feeling embarrassed.

After a few days, the stork invited the fox to dinner. When the fox arrived, the stork welcomed him and served the dinner in a long-necked jar with a narrow mouth.

The stork replied, "I prepared some special meat for you, my friend. Enjoy your dinner."

The fox tried to fetch the piece of meat from the jar, but could only lick the top. After a while, the hungry fox left feeling irritated and embarrassed.

Moral

People will treat you the same way as you treat them.

The Hare and the Tortoise

A hare in the jungle always made fun of the tortoise and called him the slowest runner in the world. One day, the tortoise was tired of the bullying and said, "I will defeat you in a race."

The hare laughed and accepted the challenge.

The race began, and the tortoise started walking at a slow pace while the hare ran with speed. After a while, the hare stopped and looked back but could not spot the tortoise. Feeling confident, the hare decided to rest and fell asleep. The tortoise kept walking and overtook the hare. The hare woke up and was shocked to see the tortoise approaching the finish line.

He ran as fast as he could, but the tortoise crossed the finish line and won the race. The humbled hare never made fun of the tortoise again.

Moral

Slow and steady wins the race.

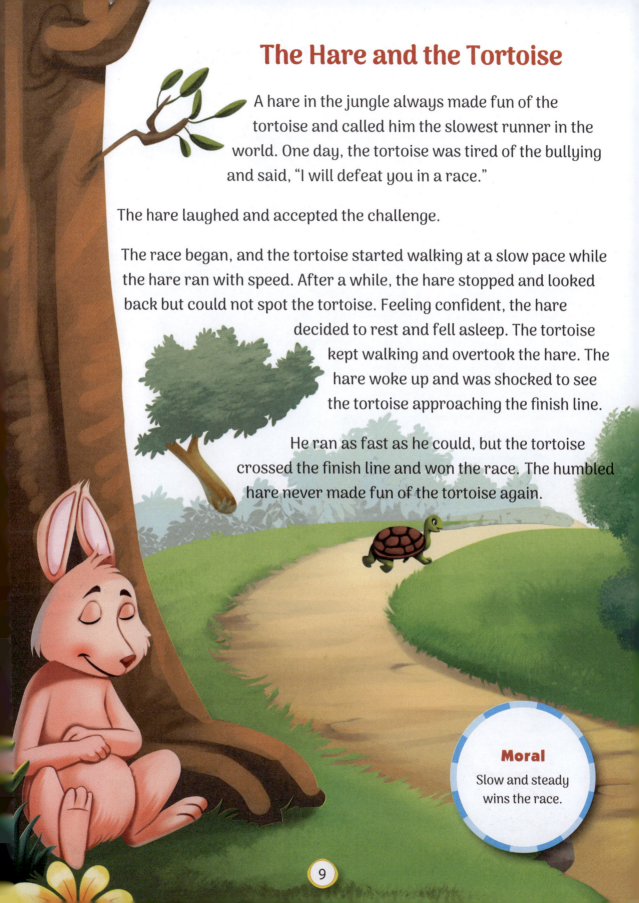

The Ant and the Dove

One day, an ant fell into the river and was drowning. A dove saw the ant and decided to help him. She dropped a leaf in the water. The ant stepped on the leaf. The dove then carried the leaf back and placed it gently on the ground. The ant crawled to safety.

"Thank you so much. I will always remember this," said the ant.

After a few days, the ant saw a hunter. When she saw the hunter pointing an arrow at the dove, she was terrified. To save the dove, the ant immediately ran towards the hunter and bit his toe.

"Ouch!" screamed out the man, losing concentration as he shot the arrow. The arrow missed the dove and she flew away to safety. The dove thanked the ant later.

Moral

One good deed
deserves another.

The Ungrateful Man

Once, a poor priest was passing through a forest when he saw a well. He looked down and saw a tiger, a monkey, a snake, and a man trapped inside.

The tiger said, "O priest help me! Pull me out of this well."

"How can I help you? Tigers prey on humans," replied the priest.

"True, I'm a killer and I prey on animals and humans, but I'm not ungrateful."

So, the priest pulled him out of the well. He then pulled the monkey out.

Then, the snake begged him to pull him out as well. "O priest, we only bite those who provoke us. I swear to never harm you or your family." The priest pulled the snake out too.

All the animals advised him, "You must not help the man down in the well, as he is ungrateful."

The tiger and monkey asked the priest to pay them a visit later and left.

The snake said, "If you ever need help, you must remember me, and I'll be there." And then he left too.

The priest took pity on the man in the well and pulled him out anyway. Before leaving, the man said, "O priest, I am a goldsmith. You can visit me if you need my services."

The priest went to the monkey's place, who gave him several fruits to eat. The priest went to the tiger's den. The tiger gifted him a gold necklace and said, "Once, I killed a prince. He was wearing this necklace. You can take it."

The priest then visited the goldsmith and showed him the necklace and told him about the tiger's story.

The goldsmith recognised the necklace he had made for the missing prince. He went to the king's palace and provoked the king into believing that the priest had killed the prince and stolen his necklace.

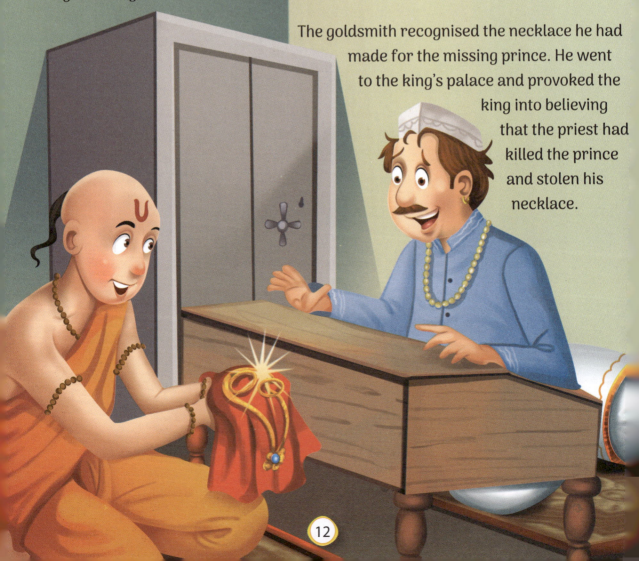

The angry king ordered his soldiers to arrest the priest and execute him before sunrise. The soldiers threw the priest into the dungeon. The priest summoned the snake and asked it for help.

"I will bite the queen. Nothing will be able to cure her except your touch," said the snake and left.

The snake bit the queen. The royal physicians could not heal her. The king was surprised to hear that the priest could help the queen. He set the priest free, who cured the queen with a single touch.

The king was grateful to the priest and asked him to explain his story. The priest narrated the entire incident to him.

The king believed him and rewarded him and his family. He threw the goldsmith into prison for lying about the theft and for betraying the priest.

Moral

Never betray the trust of others.

13

The Swan and the Owl

A beautiful swan lived near a lake at the edge of the forest. One day, an owl saw the swan swimming gracefully across the lake and praised him. Soon they became friends and spent a lot of time together. One day, the owl said, "I am bored of this place. I must go back to my home near the lotus grove in the forest. Please visit my house any time you want."

A few days later, the swan went to meet the owl. Since it was daytime, the owl did not come out of its hole and asked the swan to wait for night. The swan was disappointed. Tired from his journey, the swan slept near a tree.

At dawn, a group of merchants was passing by singing hymns. The owl replied with a loud and harsh hoot and hid in his hole. Considering it a bad omen, an angry merchant shot an arrow at the owl, but it hit the swan instead and killed it instantly.

Moral

Choose your friends wisely.

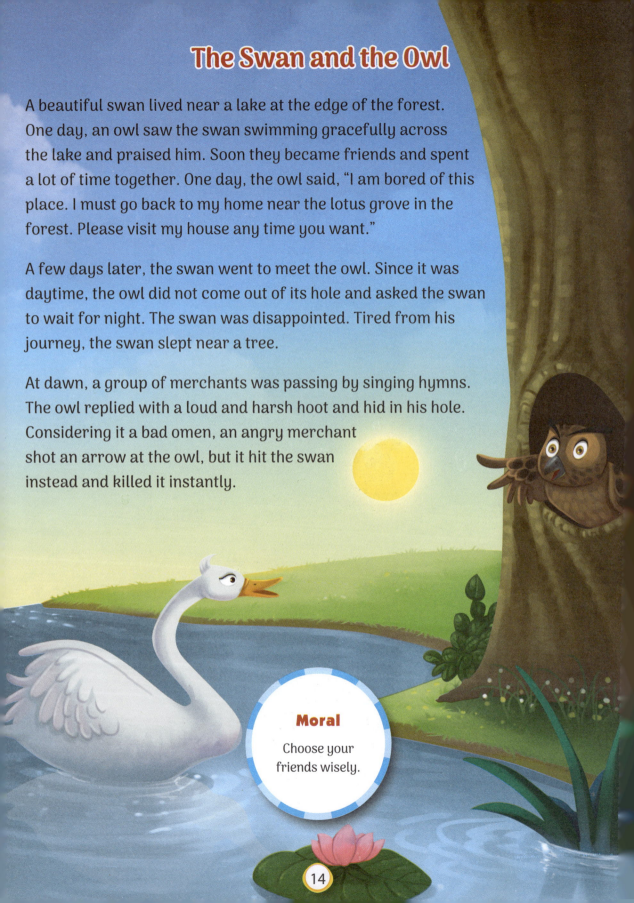

The Wise Gander

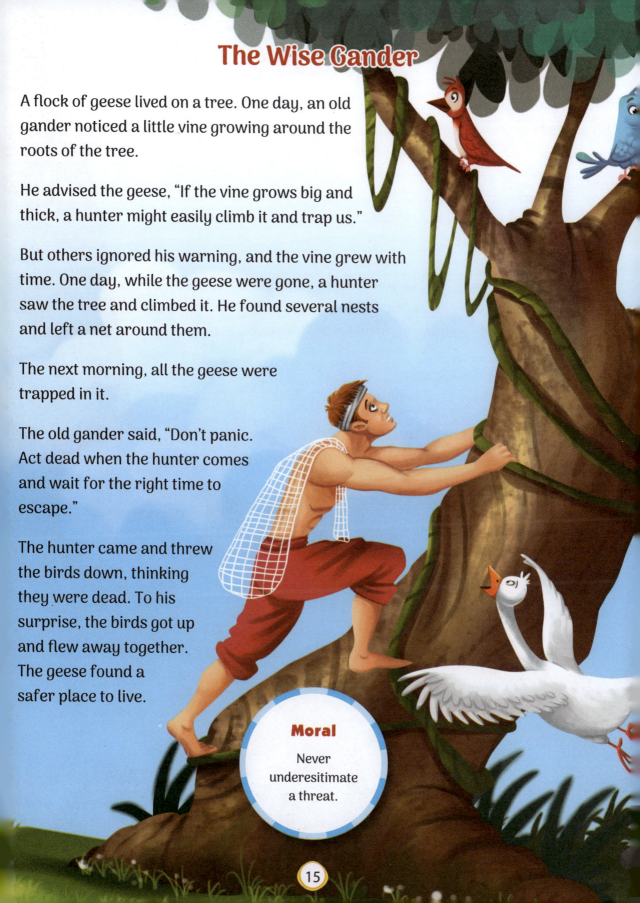

A flock of geese lived on a tree. One day, an old gander noticed a little vine growing around the roots of the tree.

He advised the geese, "If the vine grows big and thick, a hunter might easily climb it and trap us."

But others ignored his warning, and the vine grew with time. One day, while the geese were gone, a hunter saw the tree and climbed it. He found several nests and left a net around them.

The next morning, all the geese were trapped in it.

The old gander said, "Don't panic. Act dead when the hunter comes and wait for the right time to escape."

The hunter came and threw the birds down, thinking they were dead. To his surprise, the birds got up and flew away together. The geese found a safer place to live.

Moral

Never underesitimate a threat.

The Lion and the Ram

Once, a ram was separated from his flock in a forest. He had big horns and did not fear anyone. He roamed the forest without a care. One day, a lion saw him and thought, "He looks healthy and extraordinary too! He is not scared of my presence."

The lion feared the ram and avoided meeting him. The ram moved freely in the forest.

A few days later, a jackal approached the lion and said, "O mighty lion, the ram you fear can barely harm you. I saw him today in the forest, he was munching on green grass! He can't match your strength."

The lion was delighted by this news. He attacked the ram and killed it with ease.

Moral

Appearances can be deceptive.